ASPCA kids

Pets at Work
PAW PALS

Chance's Choice

studio fun
INTERNATIONAL

Studio Fun International
An imprint of Printers Row Publishing Group
A division of Readerlink Distribution Services, LLC
10350 Barnes Canyon Road, Suite 100, San Diego, CA 92121
www.studiofun.com

Written by Brenda Scott Royce
Illustrated by Colleen Madden
Designed by Candace Warren

Printers Row Publishing Group is a division of
Readerlink Distribution Services, LLC.
Studio Fun International is a registered trademark of
Readerlink Distribution Services, LLC. All rights reserved.

All notations of errors or omissions should be addressed to
Studio Fun International, Editorial Department, at the above address.

ISBN 978-0-7944-4108-1
Manufactured, printed, and assembled in Guangzhou, China.
First printing, January 2019. GD/01/19
23 22 21 20 19 1 2 3 4 5

Library of Congress Cataloging-in-Publication Data is available on request.

5-7% of the purchase price will be donated to
The American Society for the Prevention of Cruelty to Animals® (ASPCA®),
with a minimum donation of $50,000 through December 2019.

For Henry, a real-life hero,
and his special person,
my friend Martha.
                            —B.S.R.

1

New Room

"It has more wall space than your last bedroom. Closet's bigger, too."

Meg Harper looked up at her mother and tried to smile. The result was lopsided, with only one half of her mouth cooperating. She just didn't have the energy to pretend—even to spare her mother's feelings. "I guess."

Mrs. Harper drew back the lace curtain that covered the bedroom window. "Such a lovely view. Better than the brick wall in Tokyo."

Meg nodded. Wall space and closet size didn't matter, since she didn't plan to hang up posters or even unpack her clothes, but she had to admit the view was pretty.

The wide window looked out on a tree-filled backyard and the mountains beyond. Ivy dotted with purple flowers climbed the wooden fence that bordered the property.

At their apartment in Tokyo, a narrow alley was all that separated her family's building from the one next door. Meg's view usually included the Li family's laundry strung up on the clothesline outside their window. She'd rather gaze upon trees and mountaintops than Mr. Li's boxer shorts any day of the week.

She smiled for real this time. "Yes, it's a lovely view."

Her mother reached down and ruffled Meg's hair. "You haven't started unpacking. Dad's got a three-month contract at the university. You can't live out of boxes for three whole months."

Meg groaned. "I'm tired of packing and unpacking every time Dad gets a new job. What's the point? As soon as I get everything just how I like it, we leave again." She stood abruptly, placing both hands on her hips in a defiant posture. "From now on I'm going to leave all my stuff in boxes, so when it's time to move I'll be ready."

Meg had lost count of the number of towns she'd lived in during her ten years of life.

Her father was a computer programmer with a highly specialized set of skills. Big companies, hospitals, and universities hired him to solve their networking and security issues. Once he fixed their problems, his assignment was over, and the family would be on the move again. Boston, Brooklyn, Los Angeles, London ... She used to be able to count the cities she'd lived in on two hands, but last year they'd moved a record five times in a single school year. She'd posed for class pictures at two of those schools, but had been gone long before the photo packets were delivered.

The hardest part of moving wasn't the packing and unpacking—it was saying goodbye. She used to love exploring unfamiliar neighborhoods and meeting new people. But the more she liked the people and the places, the harder it was to leave. So she'd made another decision: She'd stop making friends.

Mrs. Harper pulled an elastic from her pocket and used it to fasten her long brown hair into a ponytail. "Well, since you have nothing to unpack in here, you can come help me out in the kitchen!" She winked at Meg and disappeared down the hallway.

The kitchen was the color of sunflowers. The paint was fresh; a slight chemical scent still hung in the air. Meg opened the back door to let in some air. When she did, she squealed.

"Look, Mom, there's a doggy door!" She crouched down to examine the flap in the middle of the door's lower section. "I wonder what kind of dog lived here."

Though she'd never had a pet of her own, Meg loved animals. She pictured a large breed—perhaps a golden retriever or a husky—and grinned.

"I found a few old dog toys in the garage," Mrs. Harper said. "And I'll bet there are bones buried all over the backyard."

Standing in the open doorway, Meg surveyed the yard. "It's perfect for a dog. All fenced in, with lots of room to run around and trees to lie under for shade." She sighed happily, imagining a big dog bouncing around the backyard. An idea was taking shape, and even though she knew the answer would be no, she couldn't stop the question from bursting from her mouth. "Can't we get a dog this time? Please?"

Mrs. Harper was standing on a step stool, stacking serving platters on an upper shelf. She didn't say anything at first, so Meg pressed on. "I'll take care of it myself, I promise. You and Dad are always saying I'm very responsible."

Her mother climbed down from the step stool and put a hand on Meg's shoulder. "I'm sure you'd take good care of it. You know that's not the issue, Meg. We can't have pets because we never know where your father's job will take us next. What if we move some-place that doesn't allow dogs? Or if we end

up going overseas again? It can take several months to get approval to relocate a dog to a foreign country. By that time, we'd be on the move again. What if our dog got stuck in limbo somewhere? And before you ask, my answer applies to cats and gerbils and parakeets and every other kind of pet."

Meg lowered her gaze to the ground. She already knew all these things, and had heard the same reasons every time she'd asked her parents for a pet. She shouldn't have gotten her hopes up.

As she carried a box marked UTENSILS to the kitchen counter, her thoughts grew sad. No pets, no friends, no posters on her bedroom walls. Life in this town was going to be no fun.

Seeing her expression, Meg's mother tried to cheer her up. "It will be nice living near family for a change, won't it? That's one of the reasons Dad took this assignment. Maybe you'll be in the same class as your cousin Amanda. You two used to love playing together when you were babies."

Meg fought the urge to groan. She and Amanda were not very close. They'd hardly spent any time together growing up, and they had nothing in common. Worse, Amanda could be a bit bossy. Even though Meg was older by six months, Amanda always took charge when they were together. "I don't remember that."

"I'll show you pictures later. If we ever find the box with the photo albums!"

Meg had just finished unpacking the silverware when the doorbell rang.

"Our first guests!" her mother said, hurrying to the front door.

A few minutes later, Mrs. Harper reappeared in the kitchen trailed by a woman wearing a bright floral dress, with a matching turban wrapped around her hair. She introduced herself as Mrs. Montez and shook Meg's hand. "We live in the yellow house on the corner. My daughter, Blanca—" The woman gestured behind her, but there was no one there. She glanced up at the sky. "Dios mio, where has she gone to now?"

"I'm here, Mama!" A girl with dark hair in braids popped into the room. "I was just looking around."

Mrs. Montez wagged a finger at her daughter. "It's rude to do so without permission."

"That's alright." Meg's mother smiled warmly. "Meg, why don't you show Blanca around?"

Meg shrugged and shuffled from the room. The girl was super chatty and ultra-nosy. As Meg showed her the house, she opened doors and peered into closets, asking questions about everything she saw.

When they got to Meg's room, Blanca ran her fingers over the stacked moving boxes, then plopped down on the bed. "I know all the kids in the neighborhood. Stick with me and you'll have lots of friends. Do you have any hobbies?"

Meg shook her head. "We'll be gone in a few

months, so don't bother getting to know me."

"That's a lousy attitude." Blanca picked up a small device with an antenna that was sitting on the nightstand. "What's this? A walkie-talkie?"

Meg felt her face flush. Of course, her mother had already unpacked the baby monitor. She'd never let Meg sleep without it turned on by her bedside ... just in case something happened in the night.

It's not that her parents were over-protective. Well, they *were* overprotective, but for good reason. As a young child, Meg had been diagnosed with epilepsy—a disorder that caused her to have periodic seizures. It had been almost a year since she'd had one, but the family always had to be prepared.

During a seizure, Meg's body shook uncontrollably. Her parents knew how to help her, to make sure she didn't choke or otherwise hurt herself. So the baby monitor, while extremely embarrassing, was necessary.

"It's nothing!" Meg said, reaching out her hand. "Give it to me."

Blanca turned the device over in her hands. "It's a baby monitor!" She grinned, dimples forming in her cheeks. "I love babies. Is it a boy or a girl? Where's its room? Please, can I hold the baby?"

Meg hesitated for a moment before answering. This talkative girl claimed to know every kid in the neighborhood. If she told her the truth, then everyone in town would soon know about Meg's epilepsy. If there was anything worse than being the new kid, it was being the *sick* kid. Crossing the fingers of one hand behind her back, she reached out with the other to take the baby monitor from Blanca. "It's my baby brother's."

"Can I see him?"

"He's sleeping." Meg's stomach churned. She had to get the girl out of her house quickly, before she discovered the truth. "Let's go outside and play so we don't disturb him."

2

First Day

"Flumbergulator," Mr. Harper said, glancing at Meg as he slid his car to a stop in front of Pinegrove Elementary School. The Harpers' blue sedan joined a long line of vehicles in the student drop-off lane. As the car inched forward, Mr. Harper repeated the nonsensical word. "Flumbergulator." After a pause, he nudged Meg's shoulder. "Well?"

Meg let out a sigh. "It's okay, Dad. I'm fine." They'd been playing this game for as long as

Meg could remember. Her father would make up a ridiculous-sounding word and wait for Meg to concoct a definition. It started when she was about six years old and needed to have a medical procedure called a lumbar puncture—in which a doctor inserted a long, thin needle into her lower back to withdraw fluid. It was one of several tests she'd had after she'd started having seizures, and she was terrified at the thought of the big needle. While her mother gently stroked her forehead, her father had put his glasses on upside-down and said in a funny accent, "I'm here to test your vocabulary. Now, where is it?" He lifted one of Meg's arms, then the other. "It's not under here. Not under there. I'll have to go in through the brain."

As her father "tested" her on words like "tickularious" and "gloppledollop," Meg forgot all about the lumbar puncture. Before she knew it, the procedure was over and they were heading home.

That was a long time ago. She appreciated what her father was trying to do now, but she was no longer a frightened little kid. She didn't need to play games to take her mind off stressful events. "I'm not even nervous."

"Maybe I am," Mr. Harper said, straightening his tie. "It's my first day at a new school, too. University kids can be way tougher than fourth graders. How do I look?"

Meg gave her father a sideways glance. He was wearing his usual work outfit—jeans with a dress shirt and tie. She nodded in approval. "You look like you care about your appearance ... but not too much. Anyway, I don't believe you're nervous. You're just trying to make me feel better."

Her father put his hands up in a gesture of surrender. "Guilty. And you have nothing to be worried about either. This school has a good reputation, and your cousin Amanda goes here, so there will be one familiar face in the crowd."

"Yeah," Meg replied without enthusiasm. As their car finally entered the drop-off zone, she unclicked her seat belt and hoisted her backpack onto her lap.

Before exiting the car, she kissed her father's cheek and said, "Flumbergulator. It's a device used by scuba divers who roller-skate underwater. It smooths the sea currents, so they can scuba-skate without getting caught up in riptides and stuff."

"Good answer," Mr. Harper said, flashing a thumbs-up at Meg as she hopped out of the sedan and strolled toward the school.

———— 🐾 ————

To Meg's surprise, there were *two* familiar faces in her homeroom class. Amanda Midori—Meg's cousin—was standing inside the doorway. Wearing a fringed leather jacket over a fuchsia and blue dress that matched her headband and nail polish, she looked like she'd just stepped out of a teen fashion magazine. Standing next to Amanda was Meg's new neighbor, Blanca Montez—

the chatty girl to whom she'd lied about having a baby in the family. *Oh, brother.*

Meg's heart pounded. She lowered her head and tried to slip past the two girls without being noticed. It didn't work. There was a tap on her shoulder, and Amanda called her name.

Meg froze, then seeing no way out of the situation, she turned to face the two girls. "Hi."

Blanca's face instantly registered recognition. "Oh my gosh! You're Amanda's cousin?" She bounced on her heels as she turned to Amanda. "Remember I told you I have a new neighbor? It's her!"

"For real?" Amanda's eyes widened in surprise. "My cousin and my bestie are neighbors? What a coincidence!"

Meg opened her mouth to speak, but Blanca continued, "She moved into that green and white house on my block—the one with the giant backyard. She showed me her room and the yard but wouldn't let me meet her baby br—"

To Meg's relief, the bell sounded, drowning out Blanca's words. The students took their seats as the teacher called the class to attention.

———————— 🐾 ————————

Adapting to a new school was always a challenge. Even when a class used the same textbook as her previous school—which was rare—they were never on the same chapter. Sometimes it was like stepping back in time, repeating lessons she'd already learned.

Other times, she felt like the class had taken a huge leap forward without her. This was one of those days. The math problems on the worksheet in front of her made no sense. She didn't know how to multiply mixed fractions! The teacher, Mrs. McKay, had told her not to worry—it was just an assessment, not a graded test.

She glanced at her cousin Amanda, who was sitting next to her, and Amanda's "bestie" Blanca on the other side. Amanda had finished her assignment and was sketching cats and dogs in the margins of her paper. Amanda's family owned an animal grooming salon, and she had pets of her own. These were two of the million reasons Meg was jealous of her cousin. Amanda had lots of friends and had lived in the same town her entire life. And she had siblings—a teen-aged brother, Gage, and a little sister, Willow, who had just turned two.

Meg smiled as Amanda added whiskers onto a cute kitten she'd drawn. Even if they had nothing else in common, they both loved animals. Amanda looked up at that moment and smiled in return.

Living here might not be so bad, Meg thought. She decided to tell Blanca the truth as soon as possible.

Having done her best with the assessment, she turned it in. Mrs. McKay frowned slightly at the sight of so many unanswered problems. Just then the bell rang, and while the rest of the class rushed outside for recess, the teacher reviewed Meg's paper and discussed tutoring options with her. "Don't worry, Meg, we'll have you up to speed in no time."

When she reached the playground, Amanda and Blanca were standing near the swings. As Meg approached, she heard Blanca shout, "But I saw a baby monitor! And I heard—"

Amanda interrupted, "Don't you think I'd know if I had another cousin?"

Other students were gathering around to see what was going on. Meg's stomach churned. Her little lie had turned into a big problem.

"There she is!" Blanca said, pointing at Meg. "Well, do you have a baby brother or not?"

"No." Meg blew out a breath. "I don't. I'm sorry I lied to you."

Blanca put her hands in the air. "Then whose baby monitor did I see in your room?"

Meg's face reddened with shame. "It's mine."

A tall boy with a face full of freckles doubled over in laughter. "The new girl has a baby monitor!"

Some of the other kids joined in, asking if she had a pacifier or needed her diaper changed.

Meg felt the corners of her mouth tug downward, but she refused to cry. That would make them tease her even more. She was good at holding back tears, something she'd learned over several years of hospital visits and medical tests. If "not crying" was an Olympic sport, she'd have a gold medal.

Besides, her father's job would be over in three months, and after that she'd never see these kids again. Well, except for Amanda. They'd be family for life.

"Knock it off!" Amanda's voice cut through the taunts and laughter. "Meg is my cousin, and she's not a baby. The reason she sleeps with a baby monitor is—"

Uh oh. Meg tugged at Amanda's sleeve. "Don't tell them." But it was too late.

"—she has epilepsy!" Amanda finished.

Meg scanned her classmates' faces, seeing a mix of surprise, confusion, concern, and pity in their expressions. Feeling defeated, she let out a sigh. Her secret was out, and everyone would treat her differently now. She wasn't just the new kid in school, she was also the "sick kid." She wished that, just once, she could be the normal kid.

3

Poor Little Puppy

After school, Meg wanted to go home and forget about the day. Instead, she had to wait at her aunt and uncle's house until one of her parents got off work and could come pick her up. Amanda's parents both worked too, but since they lived above their animal grooming salon, they were always nearby.

Meg thought she was old enough to stay home alone for a couple of hours, but her parents disagreed. "It's for your own safety, Pumpkin," her mother had told her after making the arrangements. So it was settled: Each day Meg would walk home with Amanda, who lived just four blocks from the school. "She can help you with your homework," her mother had added, as though that would make the idea more attractive to Meg. "Amanda's always been a straight-A student."

Amanda's perfect grades were another thing the cousins did not have in common. Meg's grades were good, but not perfect. She'd moved too many times and missed too much school. Her parents urged her to do her best—and they were okay with the fact that sometimes her best was a B minus.

The girls were strolling side by side down the sidewalk when they heard a voice call out from behind them. "Beep, beep!"

Meg turned to see a round-faced boy in glasses approaching on his bicycle. She hurriedly stepped aside to let him pass, but he rolled to a stop beside them. "Can I walk with you guys?"

Amanda shrugged. "Silly question, since you're riding a bike."

"It's better to walk with friends than ride alone." The boy pulled off his helmet, revealing short brown curls glistening with sweat. "And it's too hot for a helmet today. My brain needs all the oxygen it can get." He looped the helmet's chin strap onto the handlebars and pushed the bike beside him as they walked.

Amanda introduced him as Drew Bixby, her neighbor who was in a grade below the girls.

As they walked, Drew asked Meg about her favorite movies, television shows, and super-heroes. He listed his favorites, too, but mostly talked about his participation in the Ready Rangers, a local scouting group. "I've been volunteering at the Grant County Animal Shelter so I can earn my Wildlife Wings."

"It's like the badges you get in Boy Scouts and Girl Scouts," Amanda explained.

"I didn't know kids could volunteer at animal shelters," Meg said. "That must be fun!"

Drew wrinkled his nose. "Mostly it's messy. I help clean kennels, sweep floors, and empty litter boxes. But I like being around the animals, so it's cool."

Meg nodded. She wouldn't mind cleaning up after animals if it meant she could sometimes hold or pet them, too. By the time they reached Amanda's house, she had nearly forgotten about her terrible day at school. Drew hadn't even mentioned her epilepsy. Of course, he might not have heard about the playground incident, since he was in a different grade. Or he might just be too polite to bring it up. Either way, Meg liked Drew, and for a split second she wondered if they could be friends. Then she remembered she'd be gone in three months, and making friends in this town was not a good idea.

They turned a corner, and Meg saw her

cousin's family business. She hadn't been there in a few years, but it looked just like she remembered. The glass storefront was painted with silhouettes of cats and dogs under the words WASH AND WAG ANIMAL SALON. It was sandwiched between similar structures—tall brick buildings with businesses occupying the ground floor and apartments above.

To the left of the salon was a vintage clothing shop. "I live up there," Drew told Meg, pointing to an upper-floor window. He waved at the girls and said, "Sayonara!"

"That means 'good-bye,'" Amanda explained to Meg.

"Yeah, I know," Meg said. "I lived in Japan."

"For a few months," Amanda conceded. "I've been Japanese my whole life. My father was born in Nagoya, you know."

Meg wondered if she and her cousin would ever have a conversation that didn't feel like a competition. "*Mata ashita*," she called to Drew as he carried his bike into his apartment building. To Amanda, she added, "That means 'see you tomorrow.'"

———————— 🐾 ————————

Amanda's father was grooming a Pekingese when the girls entered the salon.

"Hold still, Priscilla," he said, fastening a tiny pink ribbon around a blonde tuft of hair atop the dog's head. Tucking the pooch under one arm, he came out from behind the counter and gave Meg a kiss on her cheek.

"Meggy! How did you manage to get so tall?"

"I was only seven the last time you saw me, Uncle Andy." She leaned into his embrace. He smelled like wet dog and soap, but she didn't mind. "Can I help groom the next one?"

Mr. Midori smiled. "Homework first. Then ... maybe. It's not as easy—or as glamorous—as it looks. But I can always use help cleaning up." He asked both girls about their day at school before sending them upstairs to do their homework. "Your Mom just left to pick Willow up from daycare," he told Amanda, "and Gage is having dinner at a friend's house. There's fruit salad in the fridge if you get hungry."

An hour later, Amanda had finished all her homework while Meg was still struggling with math.

"It's easy," Amanda said. Her sleek black hair fell in front of her face as she leaned over Meg's notebook. "First you have to convert the mixed fractions to improper fractions. Multiply the denominator by the whole number, and add that to the numerator. Put the result here, above the denominator." She pointed with the tip of her pencil. "Then multiply the numerators, multiply the denominators, and simplify. Got it?"

Meg blinked, trying to keep up with her cousin's rapid-fire instructions. Amanda made everything look effortless. "Yeah, sure."

By the time they went back downstairs to the salon, it was past closing time. Meg was disappointed to learn that all the animals had already been picked up by their owners. Mr. Midori had cleaned and disinfected the grooming stations and was mopping the floor. "You can help Amanda close up," he told Meg.

While Amanda locked the salon door and slid the security deadbolts into place, Meg flipped the sign in the window from OPEN to CLOSED.

As she did so, she heard a faint bark coming from outside the store. Thinking they might have a last-minute customer—and that her uncle might allow her to help with the grooming—she called to Amanda, "Wait! Someone's coming with a dog. A customer, I think."

Amanda looked through the glass door and shook her head. "There's no one out there."

The barking grew louder. Now Amanda heard it, too. She unlocked the door and peered outside. "It *is* a dog! And it's all alone." She called to her father

and went outside to investigate. "C'mon!"

Meg followed Amanda onto the sidewalk and gasped. A small splotchy black and gray dog was huddled beneath the store window. One end of its leash was tied to the fire hydrant. Meg crouched down to get a closer look, noting that the dog's fur was tangled and dirty. It needed a bath badly, but why hadn't its owner come inside? "Poor little puppy."

"Careful," her uncle said from the doorway. "We don't know anything about him yet." He looked down the street in both directions. "Did either of you see who left him here?"

Both girls shook their heads. Mr. Midori checked the dog's collar and frowned. "No tags. Maybe his owner is in one of the other shops." Meg and Amanda waited with the dog while Mr. Midori checked the neighboring businesses, starting with the vintage clothing store. When he came back his expression was grim. "No one knows who the dog belongs to. I'm afraid he might have been abandoned."

4

Meg's Big Plan

Meg couldn't wait to get to school the next day. She wasn't worried about getting weird looks and whispers from the other kids—or even getting a bad grade on her math homework. She just wanted to see Amanda and find out what had happened to the dog they'd found.

As soon as Amanda strode through the door to their classroom—today wearing a polka-dot sundress over leggings and knee-high boots—Meg rushed up to her. "How's the puppy? Did her owner ever show up?"

Amanda flipped her hair over one shoulder as she swung her backpack onto the desk next to Meg's. "My dad says it's a boy. No one came looking for him, and none of our neighbors saw who left him. My dad called the police and the animal shelter, and no one's reported a missing dog matching his description. My parents are going to make a flyer with his picture on it, but they want to get him cleaned up first."

"You didn't groom him yet?" Meg's mother had arrived to pick her up shortly after they found the dog. He was so dirty, she assumed her uncle would have given him a bath right away.

Amanda shook her head. "They want to have him checked out by a veterinarian first, to make sure he's not sick or anything. Plus, they're hoping maybe the vet will recognize him."

Blanca strode up to them, catching the end of Amanda's sentence. "Recognize who?"

"Whom," Amanda corrected.

"Who, whom, mushroom," Blanca said, waving a hand in the air dismissively. "What are you guys talking about?"

Amanda told Blanca about the dog they found. "He's a border collie. About a year old."

Blanca bounced up and down excitedly. "Ooooh, I love puppies even more than I love babies! Are you going to keep him?

What's his name? Can I hold him? What does he look like?" Before she could ask any more questions, the bell rang and class got underway.

The day passed slowly for Meg. It was hard to focus on fractions when she couldn't stop picturing the poor abandoned pup! She did better in her other subjects, however, and somehow survived the day.

It was three o'clock when Meg and Amanda finally arrived at Wash and Wag. The salon was buzzing with activity. Amanda's parents were busy with customers, and their part-time helper, Keith, was trimming a poodle.

Amanda led Meg around the counter to the back of the store. Behind the grooming stations stood a row of kennels. Most were empty at this time of day. The salon didn't board animals; the kennels were used to house the pets waiting for their owners to pick them up after their grooming was complete.

They found the border collie in the last kennel. Curled into a corner, he looked up at them and whimpered.

"He looks much better!" Amanda gushed. "His hair's so clean and fluffy."

Meg nodded. She could hardly believe she was looking at the same dog. "He looked all black and gray yesterday—but now that the dirt is gone I can see he's black and white!"

A few minutes later Amanda's mother joined them, greeting both girls with hugs. "You wouldn't believe how long it took us to get all the tangles out of his hair," she told them.

"Did the vet examine him?" Amanda asked.

"Yes." Mrs. Midori untied her apron and hung it on a hook near the door. "Dr. Vasels said he's a bit malnourished, but otherwise in good shape. She hasn't seen this dog before, and there's no record of a border collie his age being a patient at the clinic. She scanned him to see if he has a microchip, but no such luck."

"Does that mean we can keep him?" Amanda asked.

"Goodness, no! Dad and I spend all day long taking care of animals, and all night long taking care of you and your siblings. Besides, you already have pets."

"Guinea pigs and goldfish," Amanda said with a slight pout. "They're great, but it's not the same as having a dog or cat."

"He can live in the salon," Meg offered helpfully. "That way we can walk him and play with him every day after school!"

Aunt Becky folded her arms across her chest. "Sorry, Meggy. We're not licensed to board animals. He needs a proper home.

Now, you two go do your homework and maybe I'll let you take him for a walk."

Meg and Amanda traded smiles and raced each other up the stairs.

———— 🐾 ————

After finishing their homework, Meg and Amanda walked the dog around the block. Insisting that Meg knew nothing about how to walk a dog, Amanda held onto the leash the whole time, never giving Meg a turn.

When they returned to the salon, Meg asked her uncle for permission to comb the dog.

He chuckled, but handed her a brush. "He's already had a thorough grooming today, but he might like the attention. Why don't you take him upstairs while I finish closing up down here?"

The girls sat on the floor of the family room watching television with the border collie between them. Even though she didn't own one herself, Amanda knew a lot about dogs. She told Meg about her favorite breeds and their different personalities, and shared stories of the strangest dogs to ever visit the salon— including a Chinese crested that was bald all over its body except for crazy poofs of hair on its head, feet, and tail. "Its owner thought she should only pay half price because the dog was half bald!"

Amanda might be the expert, but the border collie seemed to prefer Meg. The dog was curled up next to her, his head resting in her lap. She stroked the dog's ears, and he let out a contented sigh. Meg wondered where he'd come from—and who could have willingly given up such a sweet puppy. She wished she could take him home with her.

As if reading her mind, Amanda said, "Who wouldn't love to have a cute border collie for a pet? I bet we can find him a new home."

"Not so fast." Amanda's father walked into the family room. "I just got off the phone with Sheriff Becker. By city ordinance, the dog's owner has ten days to reclaim him. He can't be adopted before that time."

"Ten days?" Mrs. Midori was standing behind him, her daughter Willow balanced on one hip. "How can we ...? Where will he ...? Oh, my goodness."

"Don't worry, my love." Mr. Midori patted his wife's shoulder. "I'll call the shelter tomorrow, see if they can take the dog. If he must stay here, the kids can help take care of him."

Meg nodded eagerly. She'd be thrilled to help care for the puppy. In fact, she wanted to do more than just pitch in. By the time Meg's mother arrived to pick her up, she'd formulated a plan.

"Ready to go, Pumpkin?" Mrs. Harper asked from the doorway to the Midori's family room.

Meg didn't want to disturb the dog, who was sleeping peacefully with his head in her lap. "Mom, look! Remember the puppy I told you about last night?"

Mrs. Harper smiled. "Ah, yes. Aunt Becky was just telling me that his owner still hasn't shown up and he might have to stay here for a while."

"I was thinking he could stay with us." Before her mother could protest, Meg continued. "I know we can't keep him forever because of Dad's job, but what if he just stayed for a while? Until he can be adopted? We could be like his foster family!"

Her mother bit her lip. "I don't think so. The poor thing would be home alone all day when you're at school and Dad and I are at work. Who would take him for walks? And the landlord doesn't want us to have pets; he said the last tenants' dog scratched up the back door and dug holes all over the yard."

Meg's face fell. She gently removed the dog's head from her lap and stood to leave. "I'll go get my books," she said before slinking from the room.

Later that night she learned the real reason for her mother's refusal. With her thoughts occupied by the puppy, she'd been unable to sleep. She got up to get a glass of water, but she stopped in the hallway outside her parents' bedroom when she heard them talking about the dog.

"It breaks my heart to see her so sad," her mother was saying, "but I just can't do it. When I'm not at work, I take Meg to her appointments and keep track of her medications and worry about her having another seizure. I don't have the energy

to take care of another living creature."

Meg didn't wait to hear her father's reply. She tiptoed back to her room, not wanting them to know she'd been eavesdropping. And more importantly, not wanting them to hear her cry.

5

Second Chance

"You got rocks in your pockets?" Drew asked, looking over his shoulder at Meg.

"What?" Meg eyed him quizzically. She didn't have anything in her pockets. Especially not rocks.

"Something's weighing you down."

Finally catching his meaning, Meg quickened her pace. She'd fallen several steps behind Drew and Amanda. The three kids had walked home from school together every day for the last week. They usually chatted nonstop along the way, but today Meg had been silent—and slow-footed. "Sorry," she said. "I'm feeling a little … oogry."

Amanda made a face. "Oogry? That is not a word in the English language. And I'm pretty sure it's not Japanese either."

"My Dad and I play a game where we make up words. *Oogry* is one of my favorites. It describes that feeling when you're not sick and not sad, but you're not quite feeling right, either."

Drew nodded. "When I feel that way, my mom says I got up on the wrong side of the bed."

Amanda patted Meg's shoulder. "Are you feeling 'oogry' because Chance is leaving today?"

They had nicknamed the border collie Chance, short for Second Chance, because they were determined to help him find a new home—and a second chance at happiness. It had been three days since the dog had been abandoned, and no one had come forward to claim him. Mr. and Mrs. Midori had decided to take the dog to the Grant County Animal Shelter, where he'd stay for the remainder of the ten-day waiting period. After that time, he'd be put up for adoption.

"Yes, I think so," Meg admitted. She'd grown attached to Chance and hated to see him go—even if she knew it was for the best. The people at the shelter were experts at matching animals with the right owners. She knew whoever adopted Chance would be very lucky. "I'm going to miss seeing him every day after school."

Amanda agreed. "I'll miss him, too—even though he likes you best."

A smile teased at the corners of Meg's mouth. It was true that while all three kids had been helping take care of Chance, the dog seemed to prefer Meg, always staying by her side if he had a choice. Still, she didn't want her cousin to feel bad, so she said, "Dogs don't play favorites."

"You really don't know much about dogs, do you?" Drew teased. "They may love everyone but they usually have one special person. Maybe you're Chance's special person."

That thought should have cheered Meg, but instead it made her sad. "I hope not, since I can't adopt him. His new owner should be that person."

A woman was exiting the salon with two Bassett hounds when they arrived. "Hi Mrs. Watkins," Amanda said, bending to pat the dogs on their freshly groomed heads. "Lola and Binkie look very pretty today."

Inside the store, they found Mr. Midori pushing a mop through the lobby. "Since we have no more appointments scheduled, I decided to close up early," he told them. "We'll all go to the shelter together." He turned to Drew and Meg. "Why don't you two get Chance ready to go? Amanda will help me close the salon."

Meg dropped her backpack onto the counter and followed Drew back to the row of kennels.

Saying goodbye was always difficult. Saying goodbye to a dog was even worse, Meg decided as she hugged Chance around his neck and buried her face in his soft fur. The dog couldn't possibly understand what was going on. He'd already been abandoned once before. What would he think when they dropped him off at the shelter and walked away? She pictured Chance in unfamiliar surroundings—confused by all the new sights, sounds, and smells of the shelter, and unable to be comforted by the people he'd come to know and trust. The thought made her feel light-headed.

"I'll keep an eye on him, you know," Drew told her. They were sitting on the steps in front of Drew's apartment building, next door to the salon. "I volunteer at the shelter on Saturdays. You can come visit him, too. At least, until he gets adopted."

Meg straightened. "Thank you, Drew. You're a good—" the word *friend* was on her mind, but remembering her no-friends rule she said, "person." As she stroked Chance she noticed her hand was shaking. She took a deep breath to steady her nerves, then stood and wrapped Chance's leash around her wrist. "Do you mind if I take him for a walk? I want to say goodbye alone."

"Sure, why not?" Drew flipped his baseball cap around and leaned against the building. "I'll wait here for Amanda and her dad."

When they reached the corner, Meg considered turning back. She wasn't used to going on walks alone. Her parents insisted she always take a friend or family member along. The dog strained at his leash, eager to move along, and Meg reminded herself that she wasn't alone. "Which way today?" she asked the dog and then followed his lead.

After they'd gone another block, Meg had the sudden urge to sit down. Her light-headedness had worsened, and tiny dots of light danced before her eyes. She saw a bench up ahead and guided Chance over to it. She lowered herself onto the bench and Chance sat at her feet. Bending over to stroke his head, Meg told the dog she loved him.

She breathed in slowly, thinking about the

weird symptoms she'd been experiencing since she got out of school. She'd attributed them to her sadness at saying goodbye to Chance, but now she realized there was something else going on.

It had been almost a year since she'd had a seizure, but once it started she knew that's exactly what was happening. Trying to remain calm, she reached down for her backpack. Her mother always made sure it contained a fully charged cell phone for use in emergencies. Meg's pulse quickened when she realized she didn't have her backpack— she'd left it on the counter at the salon.

Drew was drumming his fingers against the stoop when Amanda and her father emerged from the salon. Mr. Midori pulled the door closed behind him and turned the key in the lock. "Where's Meggy?"

"She took Chance for a walk. I was sure she'd be back by now."

"All by herself?" Mr. Midori said, his voice registering alarm. "How long has she been gone?"

"Oh no," Amanda said. "Dad, Meg told me she was feeling funny. I didn't think—"

"I'm sure she's fine—but I'll feel better when we find her." He looked at Drew. "Which way did she go?"

Drew pointed, and Amanda and her father set off down the street. Drew hopped up from the stoop and hurried after them. "What's the matter?"

"She's not supposed to go off on her own," Amanda explained, "because of her epilepsy."

"Epilepsy?" Drew repeated. "I didn't know. I'm sorry."

"It's not your fault," Mr. Midori said as they reached the corner and paused. "Which way would they go? What's your regular route?"

Drew shrugged. "We go a different way every time. Chance likes to explore."

"We could split up," Amanda suggested.

Just then they heard barking. They turned the corner and saw Chance bounding down the sidewalk, dragging his leash behind him. Meg was nowhere in sight.

They all ran toward the dog, shouting his name—and Meg's.

When Chance reached them, he spun

around and ran back in the direction he'd come from, barking all the way.

"He wants us to follow," Drew said.

They found Meg on the sidewalk in front of a park bench. She was conscious but confused. They helped her to a sitting position, then Mr. Midori pulled out his cell phone. "Don't worry, Meggy. We're here, and I'm calling your parents. You're going to be all right."

6

That Darn Dog

Even though Meg insisted she felt fine, her parents decided to take her to the emergency room. She had a skinned knee from falling off the park bench when her seizure started, but was in good shape.

While a nurse bandaged Meg's knee, the doctor spoke to her parents in the next room.

"I told her when she feels a seizure coming on, she should get down on the ground, so she won't injure herself in a fall."

Mr. Harper nodded. "We know how to help her, and how to keep her away from things that might hurt her during a seizure. But we weren't there this time."

"If only she hadn't wanted to walk that darn dog," Mrs. Harper added.

The doctor smiled. "That dog may have saved her life. Meg told me that he went to find help."

Meg's mother looked uncertain. "He's just a puppy himself. We don't know if he was actually trying to get help for Meg, or if he was just lost and scared."

Mr. Harper smiled. "It was sweet, though. He didn't want to leave her side. He even tried to climb into the backseat of our car."

The doctor made some notations on a

chart, then looked up at them. "I've treated a number of patients with epilepsy over the years. A few have had dogs who were specially trained to help them in the event of a seizure."

"Trained to help?" Mrs. Harper asked. "How?"

"They can fetch a family member, activate an alarm, help the patient sit up, and other tasks. Most importantly, in my opinion, they provide comfort and reduce the patient's stress levels."

Mr. Harper rubbed his forehead. "Are you suggesting that Chance—the dog that helped our daughter—could be a service dog?"

The doctor opened the door to the waiting room. "I've never met the dog, but it sounds like he has good instincts."

It was late by the time the family returned home. Exhausted, Meg went straight to her room. When her parents went to kiss her goodnight, she was already sound asleep. Her mother switched on the baby monitor and turned out the lights. "Sweet dreams," she whispered into the darkness.

———————— 🐾 ————————

Meg was still wearing her pajamas when she shuffled into the dining room the next morning. It was Saturday, and her parents had let her sleep in. She could tell they'd been up for a while already; the coffee pot was nearly empty. There was a platter of fruit and bagels on the table, along with two coffee mugs and her father's laptop.

She still felt a bit groggy, but better than

the night before. Rubbing sleep from her eyes, she asked, "Where's Chance?"

Her parents exchanged looks, then her father spoke. "He's at the shelter, sweetheart. Uncle Andy took him there yesterday, while we were at the hospital."

"That's what I thought." Meg let out a sigh as she sat down at the table. "But I could have sworn I heard barking out here. I must've been dreaming."

Mr. Harper pointed to his laptop. "We were watching videos."

"You guys were watching funny dog videos?" Meg asked with surprise. "Did you see the two dogs running on a treadmill? Or the one where the Schnauzer sneezes so hard he falls off the bed?" She giggled.

"Amanda showed them to me." After failing to find common interests in the areas of fashion, TV, or sports, the cousins had finally discovered an activity they both enjoyed—watching animal videos online.

Her mother shook her head. "We were doing research. The doctor at the emergency room told us about seizure-response dogs, and we wanted to learn more."

Meg couldn't believe her ears. Her parents were researching *dogs*? "What's a seizure-response dog?"

Her father swiveled his laptop around so that it faced her. His browser displayed a Web site for an organization that trained service animals. "These dogs help their owners lead more independent lives."

"Service animals? You mean, like seeing-eye dogs?"

"Right. Animals can be trained to help people with all sorts of special needs. Including people with epilepsy."

"Are you saying ..." Meg began, not sure she could get the words past the rising lump in her throat. "Do you think ... that Chance could—?"

"We don't know yet," Meg's mother interrupted. "Not all dogs have the right temperament to be helpers. We'd need to talk to the staff at the shelter, and—"

Meg leapt out of her seat. "Well, let's go!"

Mr. Harper put his glasses on upside down. "Not until after your vocabulary lesson," he said in a silly voice. "Your first word is 'puppelation.'"

Meg's heart was beating a million miles a minute. She couldn't play word games right now! But her father continued, "Puppelation, my sweet girl, is the profound happiness that comes from adopting a puppy."

Meg wrapped one arm around each parent and pulled them in for a group hug. "Thank you, thank you!"

7

Too Many Maybes

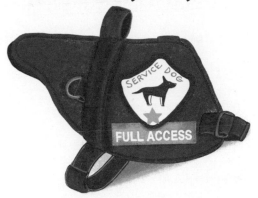

Meg unbuckled her seatbelt the moment her family's sedan pulled to a stop in the parking lot of the Grant County Animal Shelter. "Hurry!" she squealed. "What if someone adopted him already?"

Once inside, they learned that Chance hadn't been adopted—in fact, he still wasn't eligible yet for adoption—but he was very popular among the staff and volunteers.

"He's a sweetheart," the shelter director told them as she led them down a hallway toward the canine wing. "And such a looker. I'm sure his dance card will fill up quickly."

Meg had read about the long-ago custom of writing your name on someone's card to claim a turn dancing with them. "You mean, like a waiting list?"

The director, whose name tag read LETTY NOLAND, smiled down at Meg. "Exactly. I'm sure we'll have no problem placing him. After the ten-day waiting period is over." As they neared the kennels, Letty raised her voice to be heard above the yips, yaps, and yelps of the canines in residence. "We have to give Chance's original owner the opportunity to come forward and claim him."

Meg already knew this from Mr. Midori's phone call to the police station on the night they found Chance. Still, it bothered her. "But that person abandoned him! How could they do that?"

Letty's expression was sympathetic. "Sadly, we see it all the time. There are many reasons why people choose to give up a pet. Most of the time they do the right thing and turn them over to us or another shelter. But not always. We've rescued animals that have been abandoned in shopping malls and parks and alongside highways. Someone left a box full of kittens at the fire station last month."

They found Drew talking to Chance through the glass of his kennel. "Oh hi, Mrs. Noland. I was sweeping up and thought I'd sit with Chance. With all the strange sounds and smells here, I didn't want him to be frightened."

"I'm sure he appreciates seeing a familiar face." Smiling widely, the director gestured to Meg. "Or two."

At the sight of Meg, the dog wagged his tail and barked a friendly greeting. She placed her hand against the glass and he licked it.

"I'm glad you're feeling better, Meg," Drew said, giving her a quick hug before turning to shake hands with her parents. "Did you guys come to check on Chance?"

Mr. Harper nodded. "We've been talking about him all morning."

Letty put a hand on Drew's shoulder. "Why

don't you show Meg around while I speak to her parents in private."

———————— 🐾 ————————

"That's a lot of 'maybes,'" Meg told her parents that night over dinner. After talking things over with Mrs. Noland, they'd agreed to let Chance come live with them and try a basic training course to see if he could one day become a certified seizure-response dog.

First, though, they wanted to make sure Meg understood all the ways their plan could possibly go wrong. She had counted seven so far. She ticked them off on her fingers as she repeated: "Maybe Chance's old owner will want him back. Maybe our landlord won't agree to let us have a dog. Maybe Chance won't want to participate in the training program. If he does participate, maybe he won't be very good at it. Maybe Dad will get a new job and we'll have to move before any of this happens. Maybe we'll have to move somewhere we can't have a dog. Maybe even overseas."

She looked from her mother to her father. She knew their over-protectiveness came out of their love for her. Still, it was time for her to have some independence. And she thought a service dog could help her do that. Even with all the risks involved, she knew in her heart it was the right thing. "Or...maybe everything will work out just fine, and you two can stop worrying about me so much."

Her father reached over and ruffled her hair. "Maybe Chance was left in front of the groomers for a reason."

"Yeah." Meg's nose wrinkled at the memory of how stinky the dog was when she found him. "He needed a bath!"

Her mother laughed and added, "Maybe he was meant to find you."

———————— 🐾 ————————

Chance wasn't the only one who had to undergo training. From their first class, Meg and the dog were treated as a team. Just as Chance had to learn how to perform simple tasks, Meg had to learn how to give him the proper commands—and how to reward him for getting it right.

They'd been referred to the introductory training program by Letty Noland at the animal shelter, who also signed the paperwork to allow Meg's family to become Chance's provisional owners. *Provisional*, Meg learned, was a fancy word for temporary. It would still be a few days before the waiting period was over and the arrangement could be finalized.

The program was operated by the local university and occupied a small building on the opposite side of campus from the computer lab where Mr. Harper worked. A fenced-in field adjacent to the building was used for training exercises. With the new semester just starting up, the Harpers decided to enroll Meg and Chance even though his adoption wasn't yet permanent. Otherwise, they'd have to wait several months for the next course to begin or look for another program in another town.

Curious about the training process, Meg's parents had observed the first two classes. They were impressed by how quickly Meg learned to communicate with Chance, and how eager the dog was to respond to her needs. Part of the training required Meg to stumble, fall, and pretend to experience a seizure, so the trainers could gauge Chance's reaction to such a situation.

Even though it was make-believe, the Harpers found it difficult to sit on the sidelines and watch their daughter mimic having seizure after seizure—so by the third day they'd stopped watching the lessons.

Today, Meg was glad her parents weren't watching the training session. She and Chance had both made several mistakes. Twice, Meg gave Chance a treat when he had greeted a person while he was supposed to be "on duty."

"A trained service animal should only play or interact with others when he's off duty," the instructor said sharply. "If you reward him for getting it *wrong*, he's never going to get it *right*." Another time, the dog was distracted by the sound of a passing ambulance and left her side in the middle of a staged fall. Often when Chance did something wrong, it wasn't the dog's fault—it was because she'd gotten the signals mixed up. There was a lot to remember.

By the end of the session, she was feeling hopeless. On top of the two-hour classes, she and Chance had been practicing at home every single day. She dragged her heels as she walked Chance to the blue sedan idling at the curb, her father behind the wheel.

On the way home, they stopped at an ice cream parlor, sitting at a table outside to eat their sundaes. Even getting her favorite treat—a strawberry-banana split with extra nuts—didn't lift Meg's spirits. "I don't think I'll ever get the hang of it," she told her father. "What if I fail?"

"You said the same thing about mixed fractions," he reminded her. "And you got an *A* on your test last week."

It was true, she was finally getting up to speed in math—and her other subjects. Her parents had worried her grades would fall if she spent too much time with Chance, so she'd put in extra hours studying. "But that's different," she said now. "If Chance and I don't pass the basic exam, he can't be my seizure dog. What happens then?" She sniffled, her eyes filling with tears.

Chance had been lying at Meg's feet, but at the sound of distress in her voice he promptly stood and nudged his head against her hand. She stroked his head as he pressed the full weight of his body against her leg.

Mr. Harper dabbed tears from his own eyes as he watched the dog comfort his daughter. "He'll pass. You both will. I just know it."

8
Graduation Day

A few days later, Meg sat with her parents in the front row of the university's auditorium. Chance was curled at her feet. Her aunt, uncle, and cousins sat one row behind them. Drew and Blanca were in the crowd somewhere, too, sitting with their own parents. Even though Meg had begged them not to make a big deal out of the ceremony, Mr. and Mrs. Harper had invited everyone they knew.

Secretly, she was glad they were there.

It *was* a big deal. Though they'd stumbled at times during training, Meg and Chance had aced their final exam. Today, along with seven other teams who had completed the course, they'd be called up to receive their diplomas. Chance would also receive his official red service-dog-in-training vest.

Meg beamed with pride as she looked at the dog at her feet. He'd come so far in the time she'd known him. They both had.

A red bandanna was tied loosely around Chance's neck, courtesy of Uncle Andy, who had groomed him specially for the occasion. Meg's outfit—gray capris topped with a green and white palm tree print top—had been selected by Amanda, who said Meg was hopeless when it came to fashion. The finishing touch,

a silver necklace with a charm in the shape of a dog's bone, was a gift from the whole family. Chance's name was engraved on the charm. Meg had never cared for jewelry before, but she knew the necklace would always be one of her most prized possessions.

One by one her classmates were called to the stage, along with their pet partners. When she heard her name, Meg took a deep breath, trying to calm the butterflies in her stomach. Then she and Chance made their way onto the stage.

After the ceremony, everyone gathered at the Harpers' home. A banner reading CONGRATULATIONS MEG AND CHANCE hung on the fence that bordered the backyard;

string lights and streamers dangled from the trees. Her father flipped burgers and hot dogs on the grill, while her mother passed out cold beverages and took photographs of all the guests.

Meg showed their guests around the house, always pointing out the doggy door that led from the kitchen to the backyard. "It's the perfect size for Chance. Even when he's fully grown, he'll fit through."

"Looks like it was meant to be," said Blanca's mother, Mrs. Montez.

"You should see Meg's room," Blanca said. "She's got a great big closet and a big window looking out on the yard, and . . . " She trailed off, leading her mother down the hallway as though she was a tour guide in a museum.

Letty Noland arrived just as they were cutting the cake. "Sorry I couldn't make it to the ceremony," she told Meg and her parents. "I had a very busy day at the shelter. But I wanted to stop by in person to give you the good news. The ten-day waiting period is over, and the conditions of Chance's adoption have been lifted. Your home already passed inspection, and all your paperwork is in order. We were just waiting on the final police report, and it arrived this afternoon. Congratulations, Chance is now an official member of the family!"

Everyone applauded, and Mr. Harper swooped Meg off her feet and twirled her around. Chance barked and wagged his tail in concert with the cheering crowd.

When her parents came to Meg's room that night to tuck her in, Chance was curled on a cushion on the floor beside the bed. Mr. Harper picked up the baby monitor from its usual spot on the nightstand and clicked off the power switch. "Guess you won't be needing this anymore."

Meg smiled up at her parents then turned onto her side. Her faithful companion by her side, she slept peacefully through the night.

9

Home Sweet Home

"Ventrificulum." Meg put her hands on her hips and looked up at her father. They were standing in front of the house. Meg and Chance had worked hard for the last eight weeks—the full assistance dog certification course was rigorous, and Meg had spent nearly all her free time practicing with Chance. But their hard work paid off—Chance passed the course with flying colors. Chance had his new vest on, and Meg was holding his leash. They were about to go on their first solo walk around their neighborhood.

Mr. Harper shook his head. "It's okay, Meg, I'm fine."

"You don't look fine. You seem awfully nervous." She glanced up at her mother. "You too, Mom. Ventrificulum?"

Meg's mother seldom joined in their nonsensical vocabulary game; her improvisational skills weren't nearly as good as theirs. But this morning she played along. "Ventri-what? Well, it sounds like it could be related to the heart. Yes, it's that little piece of your heart that your daughter takes with her when she leaves the house all by herself."

She gave Meg a quick hug and added, "And I'd like mine back in less than thirty minutes."

Meg glanced at her watch, and she and Chance set off down the sidewalk.

A few blocks away, they came upon a park. The family had driven past it many times, but they'd never stopped. It looked nice, with trails winding through rolling green hills, and a duck pond off to one side. Meg guided Chance down one of the trails, eventually coming to a basketball court where a group of kids were playing a game. She smiled as one of them, a tall boy with freckles, sank a jump shot without hitting the rim. *Whoosh.* He high-fived his friends and then saw Meg.

"Hey! It's the new kid!"

Meg recognized him from school—one of the boys who'd teased her for having a baby monitor. A few of his friends looked familiar, too. One of the girls had asked her if she needed her diaper changed. She tugged at Chance's leash and whispered, "Let's go, boy."

"Wait up!" the tall boy shouted, but Meg and Chance ran down the path, not slowing until they reached the other side of the park. Her heart was racing and she needed to catch her breath, so she led Chance over to a bench. She removed a water bottle from her backpack and took a sip, pouring the rest into a bowl she carried for Chance. While the dog lapped up the water, Meg wondered if she could find a different route back through the park—one that didn't take them past the basketball court. She'd do anything to avoid seeing those kids again.

As if sensing her anxiety, Chance licked her hand, then stood facing the direction from which they'd come. He seemed so calm and sure that Meg felt her own confidence growing. If she didn't want to be called a baby, maybe she shouldn't act like one.

She glanced at her watch and thought of her parents, counting the minutes until she was supposed to return. If she took the long way around the park, they'd probably be late. She didn't want to let them down. More importantly, she didn't want to let herself down.

She stood and took a deep breath before

heading back down the path. Head held high, she walked at a steady pace. She wouldn't let the kids' taunts bother her.

When they reached the basketball court, the freckle-faced boy jogged over to her. Meg stopped walking, and Chance stood at attention by her side. The other kids clustered around them. Meg felt trapped. "What do you want?"

The tall boy tucked the basketball under one arm. "Aren't you the new kid from Pinegrove Elementary?"

"Yes, but I've lived here for almost three months already, so you can stop calling me the 'new kid.' My name is Meg. I hate being the new kid. And I hate being teased."

"Teased? I just wanted to know if I could

pet your dog. He's so cute!"

The others nodded in agreement. One girl asked, "What's his name?" Another wanted to know his breed.

Meg breathed a sigh of relief. "His name's Chance. He's a border collie." She gave Chance a signal that meant he was "off duty," and he relaxed and wagged his tail in greeting. "Yes, you can pet him."

The kids asked questions about Chance's vest and what it meant to be a service dog. As she and Chance walked home from the park, she thought about how her feelings about her new town and her new school had changed over the last few weeks. "I think I'm going to like it here, after all," she told her dog.

"We have news," Meg's mother announced when they walked through the door. "Your dad was offered a job. A good one!"

"Oh." Meg tried to hide her disappointment. She'd just come around to liking her new town, and now they were leaving? And what about Chance? He was part of the family now. They wouldn't move someplace that didn't allow pets, would they? Her parents looked so happy she didn't want to bring them down with her worrying. So she tried to look at the bright side. "It's a good thing I never unpacked my boxes from the last time. I'm ready to go."

"It's time you unpacked them," her mother said. "In fact, let's do it tonight. I'll help you."

Meg was confused. "But ... you just said that we're moving."

"No," her mother corrected. "I said your father got a new job."

Mr. Harper nodded, breaking into a huge grin. "They want me to teach computer programming at the college. A permanent position. Looks like we're home."

10
Project PAW

Meg shared the good news with Amanda and Blanca the next day at school. They were seated together in the cafeteria. "Looks like you're going to be stuck with me for a long time," she told her cousin, who said "I'll deal with it." The three girls laughed.

Drew Bixby approached with his tray and gestured to an empty chair. "This seat taken?"

Amanda moved her tray over to make room

for Drew, who looked under the table before sitting. "Where's Chance?" he asked.

"At home," Meg responded. "He's not going to come to school with me every day. My parents and the school think that would be too much of a distraction for the other students. Besides, I only need him when I'm doing things on my own, or in stressful situations."

"But he's so awesome," Blanca chimed in. "He should come to school so everyone can see what he can do."

"I know!" Amanda slapped one hand on the table, like she was calling a meeting to attention. Meg noticed she sometimes did that when she had a good idea. "We'll put on an assembly."

"About Chance?" Meg asked.

"About working animals," Amanda clarified. "Most people don't know much about them— or how they help people. You didn't even know about seizure dogs, and you've had epilepsy, like, forever."

Meg nodded, rolling the idea over in her brain. "I'd like to do something to help other kids in my situation. Maybe we can educate people about working animals and also find animals—like Chance—who might be able to help people in need."

Blanca swallowed a bite of her hamburger. "This sounds more like a project than a school assembly. How are you guys going to do all that?"

"We'll need help." Amanda pushed her

lunch tray aside and withdrew a notebook from her bookbag. "Who's in?"

Drew's hand shot up in the air. "I've learned lots about animals from volunteering at the shelter. I'd love to help."

"Me too," Blanca said. "I don't know much about animals, but I like doing things with my friends."

"Friends," Meg repeated. "We *are* friends, aren't we?" She remembered the "no friends" rule she'd made upon arriving in this town and felt silly. She may not have been looking for friends, but they'd found her—and she wouldn't have it any other way.

"Duh," Drew said. "Do we need a name for our project?"

"Working on it," Amanda said, looking up

from her notebook. Even though Meg was six months older than her cousin, Amanda's take-charge attitude made her a natural leader. She held up her notebook for the others to see. She'd written "Project PAW" in big block letters, over a doodle of a happy-looking dog.

Drew scrunched his nose. "Project PAW?"

"It stands for Pets at Work," Amanda explained. She looked across the table at Meg. "What do you think?"

"It's perfect!"

Blanca pointed at the dog in Amanda's sketch. "It looks like Chance."

Amanda nodded. "He's our inspiration."

"It's funny," Drew said. "We called him Chance because we thought we were giving

him a second chance by rescuing him. But it looks like he gave Meg a second chance, too."

Meg smiled at the thought. It was true, in a way, that she and the dog had saved each other. He'd given her confidence and a sense of independence—and helped expand her circle of friends. And she'd given him a loving home. What could be better than that?

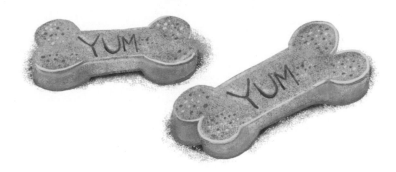

Meet Henry

Henry, a black and tan dachshund-Chihuahua mix, is a real-life medical assistance dog. Like Chance, Henry has been trained to perform potentially life-saving tasks. His owner, Martha, suffers from chronic illness. When she started having dizzy spells, her heart doctor suggested she get a service dog. She adopted Henry from an animal rescue organization when he was just a few months old.

Martha had thought that only large breeds could be service dogs. But Henry was super smart and eager to please. So, she had the little dog evaluated. Great news! Henry was an excellent candidate. Henry became

Martha's constant companion, and they went through training together. At the zoo where Martha worked, Henry had his own personnel file and volunteer uniform! The love and emotional support provided by service dogs can be as beneficial as the physical tasks they perform. For Martha, having Henry by her side is just what the doctor ordered.

There's much more adventure in store for Chance and his friends. Look for the next book in the PAW PALS series!

Cousins Meg Harper and Amanda Midori are different as can be, but they have one thing in common—their love of animals. Along with their friends Drew Bixby and Blanca Montez, they started Project PAW to spread the word about the amazing abilities of working animals. In *One Wordy Bird*, the kids—now known as the Paw Pals— get their first real assignment.

———————— 🐾 ————————

Mr. Henderson the librarian wants to find a dog who can visit the library at story time. He's heard about dogs who act as "reading buddies" at schools and libraries. Reading aloud to animals is a great way for kids to improve their skills. Dogs are especially good listeners! Inspired by Chance's story, the librarian turns to the Paw Pals for help.

The task isn't as easy as it seems! At the animal shelter, the pals meet a talkative macaw and a scruffy schnauzer—but no dogs that seem suited for library life. Things get even more complicated when Amanda makes a promise she cannot keep...